A VESTRON PICTURES PRESENTATION A DAVIS ENTERTAINMENT COMPANY LICHT/MUELLER FILM CORPORATION PRODUCTION
"LITTLE MONSTERS" STARRING FRED SAVAGE DANIEL STERN MARGARET WHITTON BEN SAVAGE RICK DUCOMMUN
FRANK WHALEY AND HOWIE MANDEL AS MAURICE SUPERVISOR GARY GOETZMAN AND SHARON BOYLE DIRECTOR OF PHOTOGRAPHY DICK BUSH B.S.C.
MUSIC BY DAVID NEWMAN SUPERVISING PRODUCER JACK GROSSBERG EXECUTIVE PRODUCERS MITCHELL CANNOLD AND DORI BERINSTEIN WASSERMAN
WRITTEN BY TERRY ROSSIO & TED ELLIOT PRODUCED BY ANDREW LICHT JEFFREY MUELLER JOHN DAVIS DIRECTED BY RICHARD GREENBERG

VESTRON
PICTURES

A novelization by B. B. Hiller & Neil W. Hiller
Based on the motion picture written by Terry Rossio & Ted Elliot

SCHOLASTIC INC.
New York Toronto London Auckland Sydney

ISBN 0-590-42741-5

12 11 10 9 8 7 6 5 4 3 2   9/8 0 1 2 3 4/9

Printed in the U.S.A.   28

First Scholastic printing, August 1989

for Emmons and Andrew

LITTLE MONSTERS

1

Nothing was going right for Brian Stevenson. Nothing.

He didn't like his new house, his new school, his new room, his new friends. He didn't like his little brother, Eric . . . and today he wasn't even especially fond of his parents.

"Well, Brian," his father spoke sternly at the breakfast table. "I hope whatever you watched on TV last night was worth your allowance and two weeks of TV!"

It hadn't been. He had tiptoed downstairs to watch the midnight creep show movie but it had been canceled for a "special" about the Tasmanian Coral Reef.

"I didn't watch *anything*," he said truthfully.

"Nobody but you eats peanut butter and onion sandwiches," his father said. "You left yours in the living room."

He had done that. He'd left it behind when he'd heard Eric start yelling in his bedroom, and his parents had jumped out of bed to see what was the matter. Eric had claimed there was a monster under his bed. If there was a monster under Eric's bed, Brian hoped it would eat him tonight.

Glumly, Brian stabbed at his scrambled eggs. They were overcooked.

"What's this?!" Mrs. Stevenson demanded. Brian and Eric looked up. Their mother was holding a gooey ice-cream container that had spent the night in the cupboard, melting.

"Not me!' Eric piped up.

"Me, neither!" said Brian.

Their parents didn't believe either of them.

"You didn't do it, just like you didn't leave the sandwich in the living room, is that right, Brian?"

"I did leave the sandwich there," Brian said. "I just didn't watch any TV. And I didn't put the ice cream in the cupboard."

That didn't convince his father at all. "Brian, you're old enough to know the difference between right and wrong. Start acting like it."

There was no point in arguing.

While Brian cleared the table, his father put on his coat and hurried out the door.

Now that they were living out of the city, it seemed that everybody but Brian was always in a hurry. His father had to hurry to work and his mother was in a terrible hurry to redecorate the house. Eric was in a hurry to make friends and have a good time. Brian couldn't think of anything worth hurrying for.

Brian watched Eric bounce out of the house to the alley that led to the school bus stop. Eric's new best friend, Todd, was already waiting for him.

Brian shrugged into his jacket and slipped his backpack onto his shoulders. Then he sat down on the stairs. His mother sat down next to him. He had a great idea.

"Mom, can I stay home from school today?" he asked.

She put her arm across his shoulders and hugged him a little. "It's not easy being the new kid, is it?" she asked. He shook his head glumly. Maybe she really did understand. "Well, you'll make friends soon," she said. They sat quietly for a few seconds. Then his mother spoke again. "Say, doesn't Mr. Coleman, the real estate agent, have a son in your class?"

"Ronnie Coleman is a toad," Brian informed his mother. "He's a base form of human life, suitable only for laboratory experiments, especially ones — "

"He seems like a nice kid," Mrs. Stevenson said hopefully.

"If you like him, you can invite him over for some milk and dead flies," Brian snapped. For a second there, he'd thought his mother might be helpful, might let him stay home. Now it was time to go.

He stood up and headed for the door. But before he got there, there was a horrible scraping, crumpling metal sound from the driveway. Then Brian's father started yelling. He was *really* angry and the first word that came out of his mouth was the very one Brian most dreaded hearing.

"BRIAN!!!!!!!"

2

"So then my mom tried to tell me that the dust bunnies from under my bed would scare the monster away. Can you believe it?"

Eric and his friend Todd were walking together toward the bus. Eric told Todd everything. He especially told him about the monster he'd seen the night before.

"And it didn't slime you. You're sure?" Todd asked.

"I think I'd know if I was slimed!" Eric said. He had the feeling that Todd didn't believe him.

"It didn't go by your desk — and do your geography homework, did it?" Eric was sure Todd was teasing him.

"Look, I never would have told you about it, but — "

"All right, all right," Todd said, changing his tone. "So this is an exclusively under-the-bed phenomenon we're dealing with here."

"That's right. Exclusively under-*my*-bed," Eric said.

"Garlic!" Todd announced. "I read once that garlic keeps you safe from — "

"Vampires," Eric finished for him. "Give me a break, will you?"

"Sure, take five. Here comes the bus," Todd said. Together, they climbed the steps and found seats in the rear.

Brian stormed after the school bus. His bike was mashed beyond recognition. His father blamed him for *that*, too, but Brian knew, absolutely *knew*, that he'd put it away last night.

It was Eric who had left it out. It had to be Eric. Now, not only did Brian have to go to school, thanks to his mother, but he had to take the bus, thanks to his brother.

Puffing, he stormed up the steps of the bus and dashed to the rear, where Eric and Todd occupied their usual seats. Brian was so furious he barely heard Kiersten Deveaux wish him good morning.

He swung into the seat behind his brother and Todd.

"Why aren't you riding your bike?" Eric asked, surprised.

"What bike?" Brian retorted. "Dad ran over my bike because *you* left it in the driveway!"

6

"No way!" Eric said, turning around.

"*I* put it away," Brian said. "Mom and Dad sure didn't move it. That leaves *you*." He pointed an accusing finger at his brother. "I'm so mad I could — " Brian tried to think of a good way to get back at his little brother. Steaming, he grabbed Eric's lunch bag and threw it out the open window of the bus just as it pulled up to the next stop.

"My lunch! You jerk, I didn't do anything!"

"You did, too! My bike, the ice cream last night, your hollering. I didn't do those things. Who else do you suggest I blame?" Brian asked.

From the seat next to Eric, Todd spoke with confidence. "The monster," he said. "The monster did it."

Brian stared at Todd in astonishment. Then he smirked. "He told you about the killer attack bunnies under his bed, huh?"

"It was a monster," Eric said with conviction.

At that moment Ronnie Coleman stormed to the rear of the bus. He was covered with grape juice and carried a mushed bologna sandwich and a dripping Twinkie in his right hand.

"Who's Eric?" he demanded, brandishing a crumpled lunch bag with Eric's name written clearly on one side. "Who's the Eric who threw this lunch at me?"

7

Everybody on the bus looked at Eric, revealing the culprit to Ronnie Coleman. The big, angry boy walked straight to Eric.

"You Eric?" Ronnie asked threateningly. Eric nodded. "Want this back?" He waggled the bologna in Eric's face.

Brian was willing to fight with Eric at any time, but he saw it as a privilege reserved for himself. He didn't like the idea of Ronnie Coleman doing it at all.

"Hey, pick on someone your own size," Brian yelled.

"Like Bigfoot," Todd chirped in. Then he ducked below the level of the seat, where he couldn't be seen.

Ronnie's attention turned to Brian. "Maybe I will," he said. With that the bus screeched to a halt. Ronnie was thrown against a seat. The Twinkie got mashed on his shirt. The mustard from the sandwich was smeared onto his pants. Under the watchful eye of the bus driver, Ronnie slunk into a seat on the other side of the bus. Brian had the sinking feeling it wasn't the end, though.

The first thing that happened at recess was that Ronnie cornered Brian.

"You're going to eat my shirt," Ronnie told him.

"I'm surprised you haven't eaten it already," Brian retorted.

The humor was lost on Ronnie. He drew back his hand to punch Brian. Brian ducked as the fist approached, and poked Ronnie in his ample stomach. Ronnie took another stab at Brian, who pushed him away. By this time a crowd of students had gathered around the two boys.

"Break it up!" came the stern voice of the principal. He grabbed each of the boys by their collars and held them at arm's length. He looked at Ronnie's severely stained shirt. He looked at Brian. It was clear that he thought Ronnie had gotten the worst of it.

"Stevenson, get into my office!"

Nothing was going right for Brian.

3

Since Brian had to share his lunch with Eric, it didn't take much time to eat that day. He left the lunchroom and headed for the boys' room, where he figured he could hide from Ronnie Coleman until sixth period. But before he got to the boys' room, he passed the science room. In the science room Kiersten Deveaux was hard at work.

As far as Brian was concerned, Kiersten was the one new part of his life that had possibilities. She was so pretty it took his breath away to look at her. *And* she was nice. She never said anything mean to him. She never teased him. She always said hello and she always smiled when she saw him.

Brian stood at the door and watched Kiersten. She was working on her science project, taking instant pictures of a cactus. The plant had bright lights focused on it, and was surrounded by mirrors. Her lunch lay half-eaten on a table.

Brian heard the familiar click of the instant camera. But there was no "whirr." It was out of film. Shaking her head in annoyance, Kiersten rose and used a key to unlock a closet marked "Supplies. Teachers Only." Kiersten was exactly the kind of reliable student to whom a teacher would give a key.

Brian stepped into the classroom and followed Kiersten into the supply closet. It was a large closet, but it looked small because every inch was filled. There were shelves and shelves of all kinds of scientific supplies, test tubes, Bunsen burners, odd-colored chemicals, and charts.

There was a whole wall of shelves covered with electrical equipment — bulbs, switches, lamps, batteries, flashlights, wires, and sunlamps. Brian had never seen anything like it.

The supply closet also had a box of instant film. Kiersten took a pack and turned around to find herself facing Brian.

"Wowww!" he said. "There's enough power in here to light up Yankee Stadium."

She ignored his remark. "Already out on parole?" she asked.

Brian hadn't realized that she'd seen his scuffle with Ronnie or the principal's reaction to it. He changed the subject. "What are you working on?" he asked, following her back to her cactus.

While she readjusted the lights, he reloaded the camera for her, held it at arm's length from himself, and snapped a picture. An undeveloped picture whirred out of the camera body. Brian put the camera down on the counter.

"It's a night-blooming cactus," Kiersten explained. She was keeping it in artificial light all the time to see if she could get it to bloom in the light.

She snapped a picture of her cactus and put the still-developing photograph on top of a stack.

"See, I'm documenting my experiment with photographs."

Brian picked up the stack, held them by the wide white border, and flipped them. "Look," he said. "You can make it be like a movie."

"Hey, time-lapse photography!" Kiersten exclaimed. "Neat idea! Thanks."

Brian glowed with her praise. "Does that mean we can team up on the project?" he asked boldly.

Kiersten frowned at him. "Forget it, Brian. This is mine. I've done all the work. I'm not about to share it at this point."

"Okay, sure," he said, embarrassed. He backed toward the door. "Well, I've got to be going now. See you around."

Kiersten didn't answer. She was already looking at the picture she'd taken of her cactus. Then, just before Brian turned to head for the boys' room, he saw her pick up the photograph he'd taken of himself. And look at it!

4

That night Brian lay in bed in Eric's room. Eric had been so sure that there was a monster under his bed that he'd dared Brian to change rooms. Brian smiled to himself. He'd held out until Eric's dare included money — three dollars and thirty-seven cents, to be exact.

He pulled the covers up under his chin and listened. Eric and Todd were in his room upstairs. Todd was telling a ghost story. Brian could hear every word.

". . . so the girl's alone and she's getting really scared. Her roommate's not there, see, and she's in this room on the second floor . . ."

Brian liked ghost stories, too, but they were most fun when *he* was the one doing the scaring. In the room above him, Todd kept talking.

". . . and *suddenly*, from outside, she hears this thump-THUMP, thump-THUMP!"

Brian got an idea. He pushed back the covers, got out of bed, and tiptoed across the room to the door. There by the door was Eric's hockey stick. It was just what he needed. He sneaked across the hallway to the stairs.

". . . so she gets *real* brave," Todd went on. "And she inches her way to the door. And she hears it again, thump-THUMP, thump-THUMP!"

Brian inched up the staircase. He didn't want to make a sound. Yet.

". . . so she yells out 'Who's there?' and nobody answers. But there's this thump-THUMP, and it's coming closer and closer . . ."

Brian could almost hear Eric's heart pounding. Even Todd's voice was shaking as he continued the story.

". . . so she opens the door and screams, but nothing will come out. All there is, is — "

The moment Brian was waiting for! He took Eric's hockey stick and thunked it on the stairs.

Thump-THUMP, thump-THUMP.

Eric and Todd were still screaming in fright when Brian got back to the bedroom door. He was laughing so hard that he almost didn't notice the eerie blue glow in the room. There were muffled sounds of static coming from the closet.

But all Brian could hear was the thump-THUMP, thump-THUMP of his own heart.

5

The blue glow wasn't the only weird thing going on in the bedroom. All the covers had been pulled off the bed and were piled up along one wall.

The light switch didn't work. Brian flipped it frantically. No luck.

Brian took a deep breath and looked around as calmly as he could. He forced himself to walk over to the closet door. He took hold of the knob. He opened it.

There, lying on its side, was the big television set — the one that belonged in the living room. It was on, but there was no real picture on the screen and the speaker crackled with static.

How could that be? Brian wondered. Eric couldn't have done it. He was upstairs in the attic room with Todd. Besides, this television was so big that even with Todd's help, Eric wouldn't have been able to get it upstairs.

Brian reached to turn it off. But instead of turning off, the channels suddenly started changing wildly. The sound went up, then down. It was as if someone were playing with the remote control.

Brian switched the television off. It switched back on!

There was a loud thunk! Brian spun around to see where it had come from. A crumpled-up comforter was slithering under the bed all by itself, and on it was the remote control unit!

They disappeared into the darkness under the bed.

Brian knew then that Eric was right. There *was* a monster under Eric's bed and Brian decided to trap it.

This was going to take some planning. Brian needed time to think.

He grabbed a pillow and a blanket and headed for the living room. He'd have peace and quiet there. He could make his plan. But the sofa was so soft, and it was so late, and he was so tired that he just couldn't stay awake long.

The next thing Brian knew, Eric and Todd were standing over him, the morning sun streaming in behind their backs.

"Hey, Brian, you okay?" Eric asked.

"Looks like you got *two* weird phenomena in your house," Todd remarked. "A monster — and a giant chicken!"

Brian sat up and scratched his head sleepily.

All the events of the night before came back to him and they were very strange, indeed.

"Okay, chicken," Eric said to him. "Pay up. Let me have the three dollars and thirty-seven cents!"

Brian knew what had to be done. He was the man to do it. He'd spend another night in Eric's room, and this time not only would he stay all night, but he'd beat the monster at his own game!

"Double or nothing," he said.

"We'll be *so* rich!" Todd said, his eyes brightening with the thought.

"Deal." Eric put out his hand to seal the deal with Brian.

But Brian didn't even notice. He was already too busy with his plans.

6

Brian had a very busy day. First he dismantled his broken bicycle. It had a *lot* of usable parts. Then he found Eric's old rocking horse. That was good, too. He used the frame and the springs. Then all he needed were some rubber bands, a lot of books, a fishing line, an alarm clock, his hockey stick, a flashlight, a pair of scissors, and a bag of Doritos.

While Eric and Todd played pirates in the backyard, Brian worked. While his mother and father spackled the living room, Brian worked. Nobody noticed what he was up to, but by dinnertime he was just about ready. At nine-fifteen, he was in Eric's room in bed.

"Brian, are you feeling okay?" His mother came into the darkened bedroom to ask him. Brian never wanted to go to bed early.

"Fine, Mom," he said. "I've got a big day tomorrow. I want to get a good night's sleep."

His mother looked at him as if she didn't believe him. Brian gave her a good-night hug. She kissed him and left him alone in the darkness.

Brian switched on the flashlight. He was really ready. The bed was supported by a stack of books that could be removed with the squeeze of his bicycle brake. The whole room was a tangle of fishing line, all of which could be pulled tight around a monster at the snap of a spring.

Brian held a flashlight in his left hand. The scissors and the hockey stick were by his right side.

He waited.

Nothing happened.

Brian ate a corn chip. Then he ate another. He liked corn chips. He thought that monsters probably liked them, too. He scattered corn chips on the floor.

Nothing happened except that Brian got sleepier and sleepier. Soon, he was sound asleep.

Suddenly, he was jolted awake by the unmistakable sound of someone — or something — munching on corn chips.

Slowly, Brian reached for the scissors with one hand and the bicycle brake with the other. At the same instant, he used them both. The rubber band snapped, releasing the fishing line trap, which whirled around the room, encircling everything in its path. The bicycle brake pulled on the big springs, which loosened the bolts on the bed and made it drop flat on the floor. The alarm clock began clanging loudly.

Brian grabbed his flashlight and switched it on, searching through the darkness for his foe.

But before he saw anything, he felt its presence behind him. Dropping the flashlight, Brian reached over his shoulder and grabbed, tugging with all his might. He pulled the monster up over his own head and sent it hurtling across the room. Then, before the monster could recover, Brian bounded out of bed and began wrestling with the creature furiously.

Just then, the lights snapped on in the room. Brian's father was standing in the doorway, with his hands on his hips. He looked very angry.

"Dad! The monster — " Brian began, but when he looked at the creature he'd pinned to the floor, all he saw was a pile of clothes.

His father stared in disbelief at the incredible mess Brian had made with his monster trap.

Brian stared in disbelief at the pile of clothes.

"Clean it up!" his father said. Then he turned, switched off the light, and pulled the door shut behind him.

Brian's eyes adjusted to the darkness again. He looked at the clothes pile carefully. There was something really funny about it. They weren't his clothes!

He took his hockey stick and poked at the pile tentatively. A sleeve in the pile grabbed the hockey stick and yanked it from Brian's grip!

Brian grabbed Eric's Lego storage bucket and slammed it down over the clothes. The clothes slammed back, throwing Brian up into the air and then onto the bed!

Brian looked up, and what he saw was a creature that looked a little bit like a kid, but his skin was sort of blue-white. He wore one earring in his left ear. It was a little golden skeleton. Around his chest, he wore a special leather vest.

Brian stared at the creature.

The creature opened his mouth. He had pointy gray teeth and a purple tongue. He began to utter a sound. He said, "Booooo!"

7

Brian was so scared he couldn't talk. He just gaped at the monster. The monster's face broke into a ghoulish grin.

"Gotcha!" the monster said. Then he smirked at Brian. "Why don't you scream?" he asked. "Your dad will come back in and be *really* angry."

"And you'll turn into clothes when the lights go on again?" Brian asked, guessing.

The monster nodded. Brian had guessed right.

"Well, then, why don't we just open the blinds on the window and watch the sun rise? You can't turn that off, can you?"

The monster looked uncomfortable at the mention of the sun, which was now lightening the predawn sky. He looked at Brian's alarm clock. He looked worried when he saw what time it was. He began inching toward the bed. Brian blocked his escape.

As the first beam of light shone through the half-closed blinds, weird little horns suddenly popped up on each side of the monster's head. Then steam began to rise from his body.

"What's happening?" Brian asked, suddenly concerned.

"Bacon and eggs, kid," the monster said. "Sunny side up."

Brian could tell that the monster was in real trouble. "You're dying!" he said. "The sunlight — first it makes your horns grow, then it kills you. Is that right?"

"No time to talk, kid," the monster said. "I got to get under the bed."

"No way," Brian said. "You wrecked my bike, didn't you? You've been pulling stuff and getting me into trouble.

"That's my *job*. I get kids into trouble. You're a kid. I get you into trouble. Now, get me out of trouble. Let me go."

Brian had no intention of letting the monster go. He wanted revenge! But as he watched, the monster's skin began to sizzle, just like butter in a frying pan. His eyes bugged out and then closed weakly. He was dying right there in the bedroom. Somehow it seemed to Brian that revenge wasn't going to be much fun when all it took was a sunbeam. And besides, at least he knew the truth now — and the solution.

Gently he shoved the weakened monster into a shadow, out of the sunbeam. While the monster recovered slowly, Brian returned to the bed and lifted it from the floor. Then, with astonishing speed, the creature scooted across the floor and disappeared into the darkness under the bed.

Before Brian had a chance to collapse on the bed, it flipped up again. The monster, now fully recovered, stuck his head out from underneath and winked at Brian.

"The name's Maurice, and I'll catch you later!" he said. With that, the monster disappeared back under the bed.

8

Bright and early the next morning Brian's father put him to work. First he had to clean up the incredible mess in Eric's room. Brian didn't like doing it, but the mess was the surest proof he had that he had actually trapped the monster.

Next Brian had to clean out the garage. The people who had lived in the house before the Stevensons had left the garage full of junk. It took Brian a long time to clean it up and put the garbage in giant plastic bags — time he would much rather have spent riding his bicycle — if he'd had a bicycle. The one good thing about all the junk was that a lot of it was lights. There was an old movie projector; it just needed a new plug. There was a sunlamp that needed a bulb. There were three flashlights. One had a broken switch, but the other two just needed batteries.

Brian set these things aside as he dragged the garbage bags to the end of the driveway, where the town truck would collect them on Monday. Eric trailed after him.

"You're telling me there are no more monsters?" Eric asked.

"Not after last night," Brian assured his brother. "Your room is monster-clean, so now we can switch again." Brian tossed the final garbage bag by the curb.

"Then what was that rumble I heard down there last night?" Eric asked.

"That wasn't a rumble; that was nuclear war. And I won. So pay up!" He returned to the now clean garage to collect the lights. Eric grumbled but agreed to change rooms again and promised to pay Brian as soon as he got his next few allowances.

Brian thought that, for once, things were looking up until he heard a terrible clattering sound. He turned to look at the end of the driveway, where the noise had come from. There he saw that all of the neatly piled garbage bags had been torn open and the contents scattered across the lawn and into the street.

Brian got to the end of the driveway just in time to see Ronnie Coleman rounding the corner on his bicycle, pedaling furiously.

Brian didn't know exactly how he was going to get his revenge on Ronnie. He just knew that he would. And soon.

9

That night Brian lay in his own bed. Once again he was prepared to trap the monster, but this time he knew his trap would work. One flip of a switch, and the room would be flooded with light. The monster would be instant clothes.

Suddenly, there was a muffled sound and the bed moved ever so slightly. Brian looked up to see the monster at the foot of his bed. He flipped his switch and the room was flooded with light — everything from the movie projector to Christmas lights. In an instant, the monster became clothes — the same messy pile that Brian had wrestled with the night before. Brian smiled to himself proudly.

Then the clothes talked. "Uh, say, Brian, how about lighting a candle? These lights are painful, man."

"Forget it," Brian said. "I've got enough problems without you running around, getting me into trouble."

"*Me* get *you* into trouble? How about my sizzling act last night?"

"What about my bike?" Brian challenged.

"I'll get you a new bike," Maurice promised. "Just get me out of these clothes!"

"All right, all right," Brian finally agreed, reaching for the switch. "But any funny moves and *you're clothes!*"

Within a few seconds the clothes transformed themselves back into Maurice. He smiled and began strutting around the room. "You don't realize it, Bri, but today is your lucky day!"

"What do you mean? Like I get three wishes or something?" Brian asked eagerly.

Maurice shook his head. "Wishes are strictly bush-league leprechaun stuff, pal. I'm a monster. Monsters don't do wishes."

"Then what do you do?"

"I have the time of my life — and you can, too!" His eyes sparkled with excitement. Maurice stuck one of his feet under Brian's bed. It seemed to melt into the darkness.

"How'd you do that?" Brian asked.

"Magic, chump," Maurice told him. "You have to be handsome and gorgeous like me — or have someone as handsome and gorgeous as me to help you. What do you say?"

Brian couldn't believe what he was hearing. He'd never met anybody who was anything like

28

Maurice! What would it be like to go to his world? Would everybody there be like him? Would it be dangerous? Even more important, would he be able to get back?

"I can't," Brian said.

"What do you mean, you can't? You can't jam a basketball. You can't get hit by a grenade and survive. Those things you can't do. But you *can* take a walk on the wild side!"

"And how do I know if I go down there I'll be able to return?"

Maurice pointed to himself, to his ugly chalky-white face sprinkled with grotesque moles. "Does this look like a face you can't trust?" he asked.

While Brian considered the answer, Maurice told him that the under-the-bed world was a kid's fantasy land.

"Think of it, Bri. No teachers, no rules, no homework, no parents. Leave your clothes on the floor. Leave a mess on the table. Tease your kid brother. Nobody will care. Nobody will bawl you out. Nobody will punish you. Are you ready?"

Brian could feel his pulse quicken. This was just what he'd been waiting for.

"I was *born* ready!" he told Maurice excitedly. Then, pausing only to slip a flashlight into his pocket, he followed Maurice.

Under the bed, through the floor. Into an inky darkness.

10

Brian's first impression was that he'd entered a real life Chutes and Ladders game. As he and Maurice climbed down one ladder, he saw dozens more around him, as well as poles and slides. They were connected by catwalks, rope bridges, and terraces, reaching dozens and dozens of different levels, all extending into darkness.

Brian followed Maurice automatically, but paused on a landing that had a pole with city signs on it. New York one way, Los Angeles another, Houston, a third. Brian studied the signs and tried to get his bearings.

"Friend," Maurice said, pointing to the ladders above them. "Every one of those leads to some poor soul's bedroom. I'll teach you about that later, but first let me show you around down here."

With that Maurice grabbed a shiny brass pole and slid down three levels. Brian grabbed the pole, too, closed his eyes, and followed as carefully as he could.

Maurice was right. The under-the-bed world was a dream come true. First they stopped in the game room. Four huge walls were lined with video games. In the center of the room was a gigantic bucket labeled "Mom's Change." It was filled to the brim with quarters. No matter how many Brian took, it was always still full. Brian loved video games. He had a great time playing every one. He beat his own best score at Monster Mash.

Then Maurice showed him the dining room. An enormous table was set with all of his favorite foods: pizza, cheeseburgers, Oreos, cream-filled cupcakes, corn chips, cookie batter, ice cream, and sugar-drenched sodas. A lot of monsters, as funny-looking as Maurice, but each one different, were pigging out at the feast. Maurice and Brian joined them, stuffing themselves full of empty calories.

"Wonderful!" Brian said. "But who cleans up?" He was looking at what was certainly the messiest table he'd ever seen, smeared with maple syrup and covered with potato chip crumbs.

"Cleans?" Maurice asked as if he'd never heard the word. "Who needs to clean? All it takes is just a little sweeping."

With that Maurice, Brian, and all of the little monsters stepped back from the table. A few monsters entered the room with flame throwers. There was an explosion of flame while they "swept" the table clean. The light from the flames was too weak to bother the monsters. In a few seconds, all that was left of the messy feast were a few ashes.

What a way to clear the table!

"Come on, it's time for assignments now," Maurice said. Brian followed him eagerly.

In the Assignment Area, Maurice introduced Brian to Schmoog, a monster who carried a clipboard and had a pen attached to a lanyard.

"Okay," Schmoog said, checking his list. "You've got a brat in Cleveland, an imp in Atlanta, and a twerp in Boston. Go on up there, boys, and make us proud!" The other monsters awaiting assignments cheered them on.

Maurice signaled Brian and they left together. They walked down a long, dark hallway until they came to a master signpost listing all the major cities in the world — and some minor ones. Maurice was busy locating their destinations when there was the loud bang of a door slamming.

A great big mean-looking monster entered the area and grabbed one of the little monsters by the collar.

"Arnold," said the mean monster. "When Boy wants something, he gets it. You understand?"

"I tried, Snik. Believe me!"

Snik didn't look like he believed Arnold at all. He grabbed hold of Arnold's ears. "Where would you like your head, Arnold?" he asked tauntingly.

Before Arnold had a chance to answer, Snik removed Arnold's head and began bouncing it like a basketball. He tossed it up into the air, caught it on the tip of a finger, and spun it. Arnold's headless body tried futilely to grab for its own head!

Arnold's face was turning decidedly green when Snik stopped playing games and replaced it on his body. He spun the head, as if to screw it back in, then he pinched the cheeks like a doting aunt. "Now remember what I said," Snik told him. "When Boy wants something, he gets it."

With that, he patted Arnold on the top of the head and strode off.

Brian knew one thing: Whoever this guy named Boy was — if Boy ever asked him to do something, he'd do it!

Maurice tugged at his sleeve and led him in the direction of Atlanta.

Within a few seconds, the two of them were climbing out from under a bed where a little boy lay sleeping. Maurice had brought a bucket of mud along. The room was perfectly tidy; the little angel was smiling sweetly in his sleep.

Brian and Maurice covered their feet with mud and tracked it around on the clean carpet. Then, just before they slipped back under the bed, Maurice gave the loudest, wildest banshee scream Brian had ever heard.

The last thing Brian saw before they slipped back into the darkness under the bed was the little boy sitting bolt upright in bed, screaming back.

In Cleveland Brian helped empty out bureau drawers. Clean clothes flew through the air.

In Boston Brian spent a good deal of time taking record albums out of their jackets and switching them. Maurice smiled proudly as he watched.

"Good going, kid," he said. "You're showing real promise."

In Toronto Brian exploded a tomato in a microwave oven. Maurice loosened the caps on salt and pepper shakers. In Appleton Brian melted chocolate and smeared it on all of the handles of all of the kitchen cabinets. And the night went on from there.

Brian had never had so much fun in his life. He got to do all the things he'd ever wanted to do, and nobody was going to yell at him. Finally other kids would have to take the blame for trouble Brian caused. Suddenly he had an idea. It was time for another dream to come true.

"Maurice," he said. "Is there any way we can make a special visit? Like to someone I know?"

11

In a very short time the two troublemakers emerged from under a bed into a disaster area. The floor was littered with books and papers. Dirty socks hung from a lamp shade. Baseball cards were scattered across the desk. On the bookshelf, books had been jammed in frontwards, backwards, and upside down and spilled out onto the floor.

Ronnie Coleman slept soundly in the bed.

Brian looked around in astonishment. "There's nothing to do here," he said. "Somebody must have beat us to it."

Maurice regarded the scene carefully and shook his head. "No. This is an inside job." He wrinkled his nose in disgust.

Since Ronnie had already done all the work in his room, Brian and Maurice headed for the kitchen.

It only took Maurice a few seconds to come up with a bright idea for Ronnie Coleman. He removed from the refrigerator the lunch that Mrs. Coleman had prepared for Ronnie to take to school the next day. He slid the tuna fish sandwich out of the bag and disposed of it, replacing it with a cat food sandwich. It looked exactly the same.

Brian stifled a giggle.

"I wish I could be there," Maurice said.

"I *will* be," Brian told him. He could hardly wait, too. This was revenge!

"Time to get you home, Bri," Maurice said as the two of them slid down under Ronnie's bed. Maurice took a shortcut to the Stevenson house and showed Brian the way back into his own bed.

"Here you go, kid, and here's a pair of sunglasses for you — you know, just in case. That sunlight can do a lot of damage, pal."

Brian put on the sunglasses, waved good-bye to Maurice, and returned to his own room, his own bed, and his own world.

For the short time he had to sleep before his alarm went off, Brian dreamed of all the angry mothers and fathers yelling at all the innocent kids he and Maurice had framed. He pulled the pillow over his head.

The next morning was hard for Brian. For one thing, he hadn't slept enough at all the night before. He even fell asleep in math class. His teacher didn't like that.

When the noon bell finally rang, Brian dashed to the lunchroom. He barely noticed as he ate his own lunch. He even barely noticed when Kiersten sat down next to him. She told him she'd finished her science project.

"Great," he said, his eyes scanning the room for the arrival of Ronnie Coleman.

"Is that why you're so tired?" she asked him. "Were you up late working on *your* project?"

"Actually, I never thought of it that way," Brian said. It was something to think about later because right then, he had something else to think about. Ronnie Coleman walked into the lunchroom, sat down at a table, took out his juice and his sandwich, and helped himself to a great big bite.

It took a few seconds for the full impact to sink in. Ronnie jumped up from the table, spitting out his mushed-up mouthful as he rose.

"Aaaarrghhhh!" he began. He yelled a lot more and then he guzzled his own apple juice and everything everyone else at his table was drinking, too.

It only took a few more minutes for the principal to arrive and clap a big heavy hand on Ronnie's shoulder. Ronnie tried to explain, but the principal wasn't listening.

Brian just grinned. Revenge was his.

12

"Y̶ou're a natural, kid!" Maurice told Brian that night as the two of them descended into the under-the-bed world. "I knew you had it in you! You're already moving through shadows. I barely had to pull you through tonight. You did it all by yourself!"

Brian wasn't sure about that — or about what it meant. It *had* seemed easier to go with Maurice this time, but could he really have done it himself? And if he could, what did it mean?

But there was no time to think about that right now, for Maurice was leading him through the under-the-bed storeroom. He showed Brian some more of the secrets of the trade. There were thumbtacks and stickpins; pots of clay and glue; buckets of dust, dirt, and mud. There was an entire shelf full of single socks and sneakers.

"Bri, I'm telling you. There's enough trouble on these shelves to send America's youth to their rooms for life. My heart pounds when I wander through these aisles."

Maurice slung a bluish arm across Brian's shoulder. "I'm getting tired of all these boys, you know? Don't you know any chicks?"

Brian sighed just thinking about Kiersten Deveaux. "Yeah, I do. Her name is Kiersten," Brian told Maurice.

"So what does this tomato look like?" Maurice asked.

Kiersten was the prettiest girl Brian had ever known. He didn't like the way Maurice was talking about her. Kiersten wasn't a chick and she wasn't a tomato.

"She's neat," Brian told Maurice, hoping he would understand. "She's really smart. She always knows the answer, always raises her hand — "

"Always has her homework done?" Maurice said.

"Yeah," Brian nodded dreamily.

"Let's go meet her," Maurice suggested. Brian told him where her house was and Maurice led the way.

Kiersten's room was neat as a pin. She lay in her bed, the moonlight streaming across her lovely face. Brian couldn't take his eyes off her.

He was vaguely aware that Maurice dumped all

the fish food into her fish tank, but he didn't say anything because he spotted something. There, on the top of Kiersten's dresser, was the instant picture he'd taken of himself that day in the science room. She'd kept it!

Maurice prowled around the room.

"What's this?" he asked, lifting a dark cloth off a box. Light flooded from the box into the room. Maurice slammed the cloth back onto the box.

"It's her science project," Brian said. "She was using a sunlamp — "

"I know, I know,' Maurice said, rubbing his horns. Maurice began pulling things out of Kiersten's drawers and tossing clothes on the floor.

"Give her a break," Brian said. "She likes me!"

"I already gave her a break," Maurice declared. "I didn't repaint her room."

Brian picked up Kiersten's clothes, folded them, and put them back in her drawers. He was vaguely aware that Maurice was up to something, but all he really knew was that Kiersten had his picture on her dresser.

Kiersten liked him. Maybe she even liked him a lot.

He sighed in happiness and followed Maurice blindly back into the under-the-bed world.

Kiersten liked him. Not much else mattered.

13

"You shouldn't have messed up her room," Brian told Maurice as they descended the ladder from Kiersten's house.

Maurice shook his head as if he were disappointed in Brian. "Never get emotionally involved with a victim," Maurice told him.

"But *she* likes *me*, don't you see? I can't wait to see her tomorrow."

Just thinking about Kiersten gave Brian a nice, warm feeling. But his feelings were interrupted when he heard the unmistakable sound of a baseball bat connecting with a ball.

"Hey, they're playing Monsterball. Let's go!" Maurice said, breaking into a trot. Brian followed him.

When they got to the source of the sound, Brian found himself in a large room that looked like a combination gym and housewares department. The pitcher, who had floppy ears like a cocker spaniel, went into a wind-up and hurled the ball toward the batter. The batter swung. The ball soared through the stadium. It would have been a triple on Brian's Little League field. But here the ball met its target, a porcelain lamp, head on, smashing it to smithereens. The crowd of appreciative monsters cheered wildly.

Brian laughed. Maurice handed him a glove. "Come on," he said.

"How do you play?" Brian asked.

"We get the stuff from up above, we smash it down here and then we put it back. It's called Monsterball. 'We do the bashing. You get the thrashing.' Isn't it wonderful?"

Brian slid his left hand into the outfielder's glove and headed for right field.

It was almost impossible to catch the fly balls. The batters were real experts. Almost every hit found its mark on a vase or a platter or a bowl. Maurice managed to snag one pop fly, but that was just the first out.

"Uh-oh," Maurice told him. "Here comes Pumpkin Head. He's their best hitter. Smashed a priceless crystal bowl with a hit that should have been an easy out. His batting average is well over $20,000 a game."

Brian planted himself near the power alley. He punched his glove with his right hand. He eyed the batter carefully. He was ready. Pumpkin Head swung at the first pitch . . . and missed. The wind produced by the force of his powerful swing set all the objects rattling. The second pitch was a hanging curve and Pumpkin Head got all of it. It was sailing right to Brian. Up, up, up, and way back. . . .

Brian never took his eyes from the ball. He backpedaled, reaching as high as he could, hoping to snag the homer before Pumpkin Head scored big. The ball slid into the darkness and seemed to be rising as it went. When Brian reached the back of the field, he scampered up a staircase, hoping he'd be there in time. He didn't think for a second about where he was actually going. And when the darkness completely enveloped him, and he could neither see nor hear the ball, he did the most logical thing in the world. He grabbed the little flashlight from his pocket and snapped it on, searching desperately for the baseball.

But instead of the baseball, Brian found trouble.

A very strong hand grabbed him by the shoulder and lifted him completely up. Brian turned the flashlight on his assailant and found himself looking directly into the face of Snik.

Snik yanked the flashlight out of Brian's hand, unscrewed it, and dumped the batteries down into the darkness below. The rest of the flashlight followed.

Snik lifted Brian up over the banister and was prepared to drop him down after the flashlight.

"He's with me, Snik." Maurice's voice broke the terrified silence. "He's the new kid."

Snik stared at Brian. Brian had the feeling Snik was looking to see where his head unscrewed so he could play basketball with it — the same way he had with Arnold. Brian didn't like the idea *at all*. Apparently Maurice was thinking along the same lines.

"Headless people have limited potential, Snik," Maurice said. "He's with me, and Boy isn't going to want him hurt."

Brian could hear the threat in Maurice's voice. So could Snik. Snik pulled him back up over the banister and set him down on the stairs. His head was still where it belonged.

Without another word Snik returned to the top of the stairs. A door opened and Snik disappeared behind it.

"Who *was* that guy?" Brian asked Maurice.

Maurice shrugged, as if it were nothing. "Snik? He's just a big talker. Gets up on the wrong side of the bed three hundred sixty-five days a year. But it's probably a good idea if you stay away from him — and his staircase, you hear?"

Maurice was not going to have to say that twice!

14

The next day Brian walked down the hallway at school. He adjusted his sunglasses. He was wearing them all the time now. Maurice was right. Sunlight could be brutal. He hiked up his pants and paused to tighten his belt by one notch. Was he losing weight?

Brian's locker was across from Eric's. His little brother was talking seriously to Todd, and both of them looked at Brian a lot. Brian figured they were talking about him. He didn't care. He reached up to put away his math book and take out his science book. He had to stand on his tiptoes to do it. He didn't remember doing that before. What on earth could the janitor have done to the lockers? Well, everything seemed a little odd that morning. It occurred to Brian that maybe Maurice was pulling some kind of trick on him. . . .

Then the morning sun brightened, the air freshened, the breeze cooled. Kiersten arrived.

"Hey, Kiersten. Dream about anybody special last night?" Brian asked.

"I'd dream about Thomas Edison before I'd dream about you." Brian smiled at her joke. Then he saw her scrunch her face. "And why are you wearing Ronnie Coleman's pants?" she asked.

For sure Maurice was pulling something. He'd get him to stop tonight.

Brian followed Kiersten into the science room and watched her put her night-blooming cactus, the mirrors, and the sunlamp on Mr. Finn's desk. She beamed proudly.

"And the paper?" the teacher asked.

Kiersten reached into her school bag. She pulled out the folder that had contained the report, but the report itself was a mangled mass of torn and chewed paper. Kiersten looked horrified. She had no idea what had happened.

Brian knew exactly what had happened: Maurice.

"I-I-I guess my dog chewed it up," Kiersten stammered, her eyes brimming with tears.

The whole class watched as Mr. Finn wrote a zero in his grade book next to Kiersten's name.

If Maurice wouldn't draw the line at Kiersten Deveaux, where would he draw the line? At Brian Stevenson?

Brian shuddered.

15

The night-light beside Brian's bed shattered.

"Hey, pard!" Maurice's cheerful voice greeted Brian when he sat up in bed and adjusted the sunglasses, which he now wore even sleeping. "What's with the light? Something personal?"

"Yeah, you!" Brian said angrily.

"Me? Your only friend in the world?"

"My former only friend in the world. You messed up Kiersten's homework."

"*Moi?*" Maurice said, his voice dripping with innocence. "What did I do to Kiersten's homework?"

"You chewed it up. You destroyed it. She got a zero because of you."

"Sorry, Bri, but I was hungry. At that moment, I had a craving for a six-page paper on 'The Daytime Blooming of a Nighttime Cactus.' Can you blame me?"

"I asked you not to! And you still went ahead and did it anyway! So just go back to your dumb underworld and leave me and Eric alone, okay?"

"Would it help if I said I'm sorry?" Maurice asked.

"You wouldn't mean it if you said it. So just go away, or I'll turn on the light and you'll be clothes."

Brian didn't have to turn on the light, though. His father did it for him. At the instant the room brightened, Maurice became the now-familiar pile of pajamas.

"Come on downstairs, Brian. We need to talk."

Brian climbed out of bed and followed his father. He knew what was coming. His father was hauling him out of bed to give him a lecture because the principal of the school had called to say Brian was falling asleep in class.

"I don't know where you're going or what you're doing, but I want you to know, it's going to stop. Now!"

His father went on a long time. Brian didn't have anything to say. All he wanted to do was to get back to his room and go to sleep. When his dad was finally done, he promised he'd be good — as he always did, and as he usually was — and returned to his room.

When he walked into his room, he was a little relieved to see that the pajamas were still there. He snapped off the light and sat on the edge of his bed. The pajamas became Maurice. He sat next to Brian and handed him the slingshot he'd used to shoot out the night-light. It was supposed to make Brian feel better.

"I heard it all," Maurice said.

Brian nodded glumly.

"Come on down with me now," Maurice said. "It'll cheer you up."

"I don't feel cheery," Brian told him. "I think I just want to sleep."

"Aw, come on, Bri, baby. Games, snacks, pranks. It'll take your mind off the hurt. We could take a look at Kiersten, maybe bring her flowers. Or we could go see Ronnie Coleman and loosen the bolts on his furniture. We'll make it quick. It'll be good for you. I promise."

Brian decided that if he went to the under-the-bed world with Maurice, he could forget about all the miserable things that were going on above the bed. He forgot to think about the fact that most of what was making him miserable right then had been caused by Maurice.

"Okay," he said, standing up.

"All right!" Maurice said, thumping him joyously on the back.

They were friends again.

16

Something about the under-the-bed world didn't seem the same to Brian that night. The video games weren't quite so much fun when he could cheat and use all the quarters he needed. The junk food tasted too sweet or too salty, or too junky. He thought an apple would be good. There wasn't one in sight. The Monsterball game seemed like a terrible waste to Brian. A lot of the vases and lamps were actually very nice. He particularly liked one crystal bowl — before it got smashed. There was a chandelier his mother would like for the dining room, but Pumpkin Head did it in.

Brian and Maurice were heading for the assignment area when they nearly got run down by a big bunch of little monsters.

"Hey, where's the party?" Maurice asked. His cohorts were all dashing for the same ladder.

"Night-light out at the Gubermans'!" the cohorts yelled.

Maurice's eyes lit up. "Just what we need!" Maurice exclaimed. He grabbed Brian's sleeve and pulled him after them. They were going to the Gubermans', too.

Maurice pushed through the crowd of monsters, pulling Brian with him every inch of the way. "Heads up! New guy! Coming through! Stick with me, kid," he said aside to Brian. "The doorman owes me."

The pair emerged into a beautifully decorated nursery. A little baby was sleeping in the crib, covered by a handmade quilt. There was a sweet mobile suspended over the crib. It had a music box that played "Peter Cottontail."

Everywhere in the room, little monsters were wreaking havoc. One was ripping up diapers. Another put sand in the baby powder.

"Give it a shot, Bri," Maurice egged him on. "Scare the kid."

"Maurice, come on," Brian said. "It's just a little baby!"

"Yeah, it is. And we have to break them in when they're young. You go first."

Brian didn't like this at all. He leaned over the sleeping baby. He could smell the fresh clean of the clothes and the powders, creams, and soap his mother had so lovingly used on him. The mobile reminded Brian of the one which his mother used on Eric's crib — and on his own before that.

"Boo," he whispered.

"What are you? The tooth fairy?" Maurice said. He leaned over the edge of the crib and did his best banshee wail. The baby snuggled more deeply into sleep.

"Stop it," Brian said. "Leave him alone! You're being cruel!"

All the monsters stopped and stared at Brian, especially Maurice.

Brian couldn't take one more second of it. He reached for the wall switch in the room, but nothing happened. He saw there was light beyond the door to the baby's room. He pulled the door open. Light flooded into the room and all the little monsters instantly became clothes.

Brian ran. He ran down the stairs and out the door. He ran as fast as he could to go as far as he could. He wanted to get home — away from Maurice, Pumpkin Head, Snik, Boy, and all the other little monsters. He ran faster than he'd ever run in his life.

He ran so fast that he hardly even noticed that his arm had turned into a pajama sleeve.

17

It was a good thing the Gubermans lived near the Stevensons. Brian only had to run across town to get home. He dodged down alleyways and kept in the shadows, out of the streetlights as he headed for home. He had to keep out of the streetlights because everytime the beams of light hit him, his arm turned into a pajama sleeve again.

Brian shook with fear as he looked at his limp, lifeless arm. He ducked back into the darkness, shaded by a big tree. Finally he neared his own home. Breathing hard, he came around the garage and headed for the kitchen door. Before he could open the door, though, he was greeted with a loud THUD, followed by a moan.

A large object had fallen out of the oak tree that stood outside Brian's bedroom window. The large object was in some pain. It was Todd. He was in a sleeping bag. Brian realized that Todd had been spying on him — or rather on his empty bedroom.

Todd pulled himself out of his sleeping bag and

snicked on his flashlight, beaming it at Brian. Unmistakably, Brian's arm turned to clothes. Todd gasped. He turned and ran away before Brian could explain.

But exactly what was there to explain? Brian ran into the house. He dashed upstairs and locked himself into the bathroom. He stood in front of the mirror and looked at himself, floppy arm and all. Something was wrong. Something was very wrong.

Maybe he was just sick. Brian checked his temperature. Ninety eight point six on the dot. He climbed onto the scale. Sixty-four pounds. He pulled out the measuring stick on the scale. Fifty-two inches. But that wasn't right at all. At the doctor's office, Brian had weighed 70 pounds and measured 54 inches. Maurice wasn't just messing with his clothes and making them bigger. Maurice had been making Brian smaller!

Brian realized he was actually *becoming* a little monster himself. That was Maurice's real plan! Brian decided he wasn't beaten yet. And he wasn't going to be, either.

18

The next day after school, Brian was busier than he'd ever been. Maybe he couldn't beat Maurice in the under-the-bed world, but he sure could beat him up here — and there was work to be done.

The first piece of good news he had was that by morning, his arm was better. It wasn't all better, but it was definitely improved. Brian realized that the under-the-bed world effects would wear off in time, and that included his shrinking and the way sunlight hurt his eyes.

The next piece of good news was that his mother was so busy with redecorating the house that she didn't seem to mind when he sawed the legs off of his bed and Eric's. She even seemed to like the look of her own room with the bed flat on the floor. The surest way to keep Maurice out was to lock the doors — Maurice's doors.

Then, when the family was all in bed, Brian went around the house and turned on all the lights he could find. The hallways and downstairs were lit up brightly. So was his room. He sneaked into Eric's room and left a heavy-duty flashlight on the bedside table.

Satisfied, he climbed into bed. He was so tired that he fell asleep immediately. He never heard his mother get up for a drink of water. He never saw her notice all the lights and switch them off. He never heard the rumbling and grumbling in the living room as the pillows flew off the sofa bed. He never saw Maurice.

"Brian!" his mother said, shaking him awake in the middle of the night. "Get up. I need help. Eric's gone."

"Gone? He's gone?" Brian stammered, shading his eyes from the overhead light.

"If you know anything at all, say it right now," she said. She sounded almost hysterical. Brian promised her he didn't.

"Maybe he's at Todd's house," his mother said. "Do you know the number?" Brian shook his head. "They live on Birch Tree Lane," she said. "I'm sure it's in the book. I'll call." She left his room.

Brian leapt from his bed and dashed down the stairs to Eric's room. There, in the middle of the floor, was the heavy-duty flashlight. It was crumpled almost beyond recognition.

But how. . . ?

"Oh, no!" Brian said out loud. "I forgot. . . ."

He dashed downstairs to the living room. His worst fears were confirmed. He'd completely forgotten about the sofa bed. Now its pillows were scattered all over the place and the bed was halfway unfolded. That was just enough to let Maurice into the house. Brian had been careless and the monster had taken his little brother!

Brian knew he couldn't handle this alone. He needed help.

19

Brian's first stop was Todd's house. He stood by Todd's window, tossing gravel from the driveway at the glass until Todd appeared, rubbing his eyes sleepily.

"Go away," Todd said. "You're one of them."

"Not anymore!" Brian promised him. "But they've kidnapped Eric and we've got to get him back. Are you in?"

He didn't have to ask twice.

"I'm in," Todd said. He slipped into some jeans and joined Brian outside.

"We've got a few more stops," Brian said, leading the way to Kiersten's house. "See, we have to arm ourselves first."

Kiersten took more convincing. Brian told her he was working on a science project. She couldn't believe he wanted help in the middle of the night.

"I'm serious," he told her. "I need your key to

get into the supply room. It's an emergency. I need some lights."

She wouldn't even let him into her house until he told her that he'd seen his picture on her bureau. Brian thought she blushed when he said that. Right then, though, that wasn't important. What was important was that she agreed to let him in.

Brian had to tell her the story — the whole story. She still didn't believe him until he put his hand through the shadow under her bed. Then she was a believer.

"I'll help you," she said. "Just tell me what to do."

Brian took Kiersten and Todd down into the under-the-bed world with him and showed them the shortcut to the school building. In a matter of minutes the trio was emerging from underneath the nurse's cot in the infirmary next to the principal's office.

"Some science project!" Kiersten said, clearly impressed.

"Imagine if there were a bed in every bank vault!" Todd remarked.

"Forget that stuff!" Brian told them. "Let's get to the lights!"

Kiersten produced the key entrusted to her by Mr. Finn and opened the closet.

Brian grabbed a sunlamp and attached it to a motorcycle battery. He made himself a deadly sun gun. At least, he hoped it would be deadly to the monsters.

"Oh, man, that'll get them," Todd said. "That's like a howitzer or something."

"You must know a lot about electricity to do that," Kiersten observed. Brian grinned proudly until she finished her sentence. "So how come you get F"s in science?" He decided to ignore the remark.

"Now just one more thing," Brian said. He shone the light on his digital alarm watch and set the alarm carefully.

"What are you doing?"

"I'm setting the alarm for sunrise," he said. "When it beeps, we have three to five minutes, Todd, and if we're not back up here before the sun clears the horizon, you and I turn into monsters."

"You mean there's a chance I might not make it?" Todd said.

"Of course there's a chance. I'm pretty sure I know where Eric is, but I'm not leaving until I have him. Are you still in?" he asked Todd.

"I'm in," Todd said. "Eric's my best friend."

Brian and Todd started for the door to the infirmary.

"Wait a second," Kiersten said. "You're not

leaving me behind. In the name of science, I'm going, too!"

Brian looked at Kiersten. Her look said she meant business. She knew the risks. And she was smart.

"Okay, let's do it!" Brian said.

Carrying as many flashlights as they could each manage, they returned to the infirmary.

Brian led the way. One by one they entered the world of darkness on a rescue mission.

20

Brian, Kiersten, and Todd arrived in the under-the-bed world silently. Brian looked at his team. He thought they were well equipped. Each carried a backpack stuffed with flashlights and batteries. Brian wore his sunglasses. Kiersten wore her good-luck cycling hat backwards. Todd wore a grin.

"It's a parallel dimension!" Todd said. "I might have a heart attack, I'm so happy!"

"Shhhhh," Brian warned him, but it was too late. Suddenly a little monster dressed in a white lab coat darted out of the shadows and grabbed Todd's backpack.

"Get him!" Brian hissed. He whipped out his flashlight and turned the little monster into clothes.

"Wow," Kiersten said. Todd gaped at the stack of clothes, too.

"Sunlight kills them. Light turns them to clothes," Brian explained. "Okay, now, here's what we've got. Todd, that's a two-cell double D, with a supercharged 35-watt krypton bulb." Todd took the flashlight gratefully. "Kiersten, that's a long-stem four-cell with a 50-watt lamp and focus lens. Don't be afraid to use it." Kiersten accepted her weapon. Brian pulled out his own hunting light. "Now, among the three of us, we have plenty of firepower. If you see anything move, nail it! Ready?"

"Ready," Kiersten said. There was a fierce determination in her voice.

"Check!" Todd said. "Now let's turn this place into a laundromat!" Todd beamed his light into the darkness above. A blue terry cloth bathrobe landed at his feet.

"Lights!" Some monsters above them cried out a warning. The trio could hear the warning echo throughout the cavernous empire. In a very short time, everyone would know. And, they hoped, everyone would stay away.

"This way," Brian said and began leading his squad toward Snik's forbidden staircase.

A glowing frisbee whirled past them.

"Bogies at two o'clock!" Todd announced. They turned slightly to their right and beamed their lights down the corridor. Once the light hit the monsters, all the trio could see were a tuxedo and top hat, a wedding dress, a ball gown, and a mink stole.

"Fine shooting, Tex," Brian said to Todd. Todd blew a puff of air at some imaginary smoke coming off the end of his flashlight.

"They died with their boots on," Todd said.

"You mean, they died *as* their boots," Kiersten corrected him. The three of them giggled, but it was their last laugh for a long time.

Suddenly monsters arrived with something as deadly to the trio as lights were to the monsters: *slingshots*.

Ping! Ping! Ping! All three flashlights were instant history!

Brian pulled out a new light and nailed one of the assailants. The others fled, giving Todd and Kiersten time to re-arm as well, but their best lights were gone.

There was no further resistance as they scurried along the companionway to the Monsterball field. But when they got to the field, Todd and Kiersten had their first look at the kind of devastation that could occur in the under-the-bed world. A monster stood by home plate with a baseball bazooka, taking batting practice. He smashed a large-screen TV, six lamps, a glass-top table, three VCR's, and a fish tank; and then, as the trio ran toward the right-field staircase, the bazooka was aimed right at them. With deadly accuracy, the monster exploded the flashlights they were carrying.

But they hurried and got out of bazooka range, up the staircase, where Brian was sure they would find Boy — and Eric. There was no more resistance from the ball field. Brian looked down at it and saw that it was crowded with little monsters, all watching in awe. None of *them* would dare mount this staircase, with or without flashlights. None of them would dare challenge Snik or Boy. But none of them had had their brother kidnapped, either!

"How are we doing on ammo, Todd?" Brian asked.

Todd checked his backpack. He took out his last two flashlights and tossed away the bag. "Ready to rumble, sir," he replied.

"Kiersten?" Brian asked.

She only had one flashlight left. "Heavy artillery loss. One round left, sir."

Brian gave her his last flashlight. He still had his sun gun.

"Easy on the batteries," he warned his troops. "Now let's go."

Together they climbed the last few stairs into the darkness, where Brian hoped they would find Eric — *and* a way to escape with their lives!

21

Brian thought the stairs would never end. But when they did, he wished they hadn't! Without warning gigantic double doors opened for them. They were expected, and that had to be bad news.

They stepped through the doors. The doors slammed behind them.

It took the trio a few minutes for their eyes to adjust to the dark red light that illuminated the room, but when they could see they found themselves in a big playground filled with playground equipment and surrounded by rows and rows of ceiling-high shelves packed with every toy imaginable.

A huge shadow emerged from the far end of the playground. Brian knew it was the leader known as Boy, but he wasn't prepared for what he saw. Standing in front of an oversized jack-in-the-box, Boy looked like a boy, but his face had the same chalky-white look Maurice's did. He was dressed in a blazer, tie, shorts, knee-socks, and loafers. His hair looked like it had been styled and blow-dried. Boy stepped forward and spoke.

"Brian Stevenson, the real boy wonder. What a pleasure it is to make your acquaintance."

He was smooth but Brian wasn't buying it. He'd learned his lessons from Maurice.

"Where's Eric?" Brian asked, cutting to the heart of the matter.

Boy ignored the question. "And you brought some playmates along. How nice."

"I want my brother," Brian demanded.

"Now, Brian," Boy said. He sounded like a school principal. Brian didn't like the tone. "What sort of greeting is that? After all, we are so much alike. If you stay, you'll be the one in charge of yourself. Perhaps of this whole world in time. You'll be the one with the power. The authority! Not your parents. Not your teacher. *You*. Isn't that what you want?"

At one time, that had been exactly what Brian had wanted, but he'd learned that in life you couldn't always do what you wanted to do. And he'd also learned that doing naughty things wasn't what he wanted to do all the time anyway. The price was too high. The pay was too little. He wasn't tempted. At all.

"I want Eric. Now!"

"Brian," Boy continued. "You are unique. Your

feats are unprecedented here. There's no limit to what you could accomplish if you stay with us. . . ."

"Enough wind, loafer breath!" Todd interrupted. "Hand over the kid."

"Very well," Boy said. "You want him, he's yours."

Boy pushed a remote control, which opened a curtain at the back of the room. Eric was bound in the bull's-eye of a giant dart board. Boy produced a giant dart and fondled it as he spoke. "I'll make you a deal, Brian. It's you I want — your grace and wits. I'll let them all go if you'll stay and be my pal."

"No deals!" Brian said.

Boy aimed the dart and let it fly. It missed Eric's head by a quarter of an inch. Eric's eyes popped open in terror.

"Eric!!!" Brian yelled. He turned back to Boy. "Let him go! Now! Ten . . . Nine . . . Eight . . ."

"Be sensible. Why lose five lives when you can gain four?"

"Let's blow 'em away, Brian!" Todd said.

Brian pulled out his sun gun, cocked it, and aimed. Kiersten and Todd produced their flashlights. They were ready.

"Four, three, two, one!"

Brian raised his gun and fired. The brilliant white light began wreaking damage immediately.

Brian could hear the sizzle of monster flesh and the howl of monsters in pain. He even got Boy's face.

But as the battle began, all of the war toys on the shelves of Boy's room came to life. A model plane zoomed down from above, firing deadly flashlight-killing darts from its mounted turret. A tank delivered a mortar round into Todd's flashlight.

The sun gun exploded and the batteries in Kiersten's last flashlight failed.

"Scatter!" Brian yelled, but he had the feeling it wasn't going to do any good at all.

22

It was more a chase than a battle.

One monster chased Kiersten down an aisle of deadly toys. She spun around to face him, pulling a penlight from where she'd hidden it. She snapped it on.

"You're clothes, buddy," she said, and he turned into clothes. But her victory was short. A sawblade appeared in the floor to her right, and, before she could dart away, it had sawed a complete circle around her. She disappeared into darkness. Her penlight clattered uselessly on the floor near where she had been standing.

Todd was under attack from some kung fu monster guards. He'd seen the movies. He matched them move for move, trying to light his flashlight as he kicked, but it wouldn't turn on. Finally, he knocked it hard against the wall. It lit!

"With or without starch?" he asked coolly, turning the kung fu guards into clothes.

But then the tanks came and backed Todd into

a dark corner. They shot the bulb out of his flashlight. Now he couldn't see anything at all. He didn't know where he was. He felt for the wall. There was none. What he thought was a corner was just a pitch-black abyss. He disappeared into the dark.

Snik himself chased Brian. He chased him along the aisles of toys. He chased him through the shelves. Wherever Brian turned, he saw Snik. There was no escape.

Snik grabbed Brian by the neck and lifted him up high. Images of Arnold's head bouncing and spinning came back vividly to Brian. He had the feeling, from the way Snik looked at him right then, that Arnold had gotten off easy.

Before Snik could do anything vile to Brian, Boy appeared. Brian could see where his sun gun had gotten Boy, and, although it was a gruesome sight, he was glad. If only he'd been able to finish the job. . . .

"I was hoping we could be friends, Brian," Boy said. "But obviously, you don't play fair."

"I haven't even started to play," Brian retorted.

"You've misbehaved," Boy said. "Now you'll have to go to your room." Boy signaled to Snik. Snik tossed Brian through a dark opening in a dark wall.

It led to a long chute, which curved this way and that through the pitch black. Brian was tossed back and forth as he descended into the dungeon of the under-the-bed world. He yelled, "Ooooooo-ooooooo!"

He was traveling headfirst. He hit a trap door, which sprang open, and tossed him into a bin of stuffed animals.

He rubbed his head and waited for his eyes to become accustomed to the darkness. When he could finally see, he spotted Todd, holding a broken toy telephone.

"Would you like to call 911 and request some backup?" Todd joked.

"Well, Brian Stevenson, what now?" Kiersten asked.

"I'm glad to see you two. Is Eric here?"

"Nope, just you, me, Todd, and one useless door with no handle," Kiersten said, pointing to the door.

The three of them teamed together and tried to ram the door, but all it got them was sore shoulders.

Suddenly a head popped up from underneath the stuffed animals. It was Maurice!

"Maurice! What happened?"

Todd and Kiersten gaped at Brian, astonished that he would talk to a monster.

"What happened was that I fell from Boy's graces — and Snik's — because of you, my fine friend."

"He's a monster, Brian," Todd said.

"Yeah, a *monster*," Kiersten echoed. "And I think he's on our side! I have an idea!"

Maurice, Brian, and Todd looked to her for an explanation. Kiersten shuffled through all the stuffed animals, broken toys, and games that littered the bin. She found two pencils and a pocket knife. She examined the broken telephone Todd had joked with. While the boys watched, she began sharpening both ends of the pencils.

"It's the same principle as the carbon lamp in a movie projector, see. . . ."

Brian saw. He knew just what to do. Using some discarded tape, he joined the ends of the pencil lead to the frayed wires of the phone.

"Todd, you crank. Brian, hold the pencils four inches apart." She looked at Maurice. "I'll slide the dirty laundry under the door!"

Then they all understood. Kiersten had fashioned a hand-powered lamp and it would make Maurice into clothes. As clothes, he would fit under the handleless door. Once in the dark on the other side, he'd re-form as Maurice and he'd be able to open the door for them.

"Crank, Todd. Faster!" Kiersten urged.

"Go, Todd, go!" Maurice cheered.

"I'm trying," Todd promised, but it was clear that it wasn't enough.

"I've seen monkey grinders crank faster,"

Maurice teased. That made Todd really angry. The anger was just enough to make him crank faster. And that was just enough to make a spark jump from one section of lead to the other. The lamp worked!

Inspired, Todd kept cranking until there was a real glow, and then it happened. Maurice became clothes. As soon as the pajamas stopped moving, Kiersten crammed them under the door.

In seconds, the door opened. Freedom.

"Thanks, Maurice," Brian said. Then he turned to his friends. "Come on, let's go!"

"Where to?" Todd asked.

"To get more firepower!" Brian said, scampering up the nearest ladder.

Todd and Kiersten were right behind him.

23

When Brian, Kiersten, Todd, and Maurice mounted Snik's stairs again less than an hour later, they were barely recognizable as themselves. It had taken every bit of genius that Brian and Kiersten could muster. Each of the three children was completely covered, head to toe, with sunlamp bulbs, carefully wired, one to the other. One flip of a switch, one click of a button, and they could light up Yankee Stadium! But they weren't ready to do it yet.

Quietly, they mounted the staircase that could lead to their doom if they'd miscalculated.

This time the doors didn't open for them. They pushed them open themselves.

"You'd better take cover, Maurice!" Brian cried out a warning to the monster who had helped them.

Boy and Snik appeared to welcome their visitors. The monster guards were ready and the planes and tanks were locked and loaded.

75

"What the — " Boy said, gaping at the walking lamp posts that had arrived in his private chambers. He was staring at Todd, Kiersten, and Brian. He didn't even notice that they had come back with a fourth member of the team.

"Say good night, Boy!" Brian warned.

It was the signal. Out of the shadows stepped the new team member. It was Ronnie Coleman, carrying a wooden tray stacked high with car batteries — enough power to light all the lights that would illuminate Yankee Stadium. On Brian's signal, Ronnie squeezed a set of jumper cable clamps and let the juice flow.

Instantly the room was flooded with millions of watts of light. Boy and the monster guards burst into flames and exploded. Snik disappeared, howling in pain. Once they'd beaten the monsters, they cut the wires and abandoned the batteries so they could make a fast escape.

It was perfect, except for one thing: There was no sign of Eric.

Brian looked around, desperately searching for his brother. Ronnie, Kiersten, and Todd looked around, too. Brian was almost too absorbed in his hunt to notice the insistent beeping of his digital alarm clock.

"Hey!" Todd said. "That's it! It's almost dawn. We've got to get out of here!"

"Eric! Where's Eric?" Brian said. His eyes continued to search the room. Then they landed on the giant jack-in-the-box. It would be just like Boy to hide Eric there and have him pop out as a surprise. Real sick.

Brian cranked the handle and listened as the tune worked its way to the climax. "Pop! goes the weasel." But it wasn't a weasel. It was Eric. Brian had never been so happy to see his little brother. He released him from the wire that had trapped him and helped him down.

"We don't have a second to waste," Brian told him.

All five kids dashed to the door.

They'd forgotten something, however. Even though Snik had exploded along with Boy, the pieces of his body had come back together. Now in the dimmer light of the room, he'd reformed. And he blocked their way out the door.

"Coleman, think you can take him?" Todd asked, hopefully.

"No way," Ronnie said. The other kids knew he was right.

"How much time have we got?" Kiersten asked.

"About one minute," Brian told her. It wasn't enough, unless there was a miracle.

Then the miracle arrived. He had bluish gray skin and little horns. His name was Maurice.

"Hey, Snik!" Maurice called from behind the monster. When Snik turned around, Maurice blasted him with a blow torch. "How about a light?" he asked, laughing, as Snik became ashes.

There wasn't any time for thanks. Brian, Todd, Ronnie, Eric, and Kiersten had to go fast, or they'd be monsters, too.

Maurice led them through the complicated maze of ladders and walkways, up to the top — to Brian's bedroom. Maurice punched at the doorway, but it wouldn't budge. He slammed his shoulder against it. No luck.

"It's too late," Maurice said shaking his head. "The sun is up."

"What does that mean?" Eric asked.

Todd put his arm across his best friend's shoulders. "It means we've dissected our last frog," he said. "We're stuck here for good. We're monsters, too."

Eric was speechless. Ronnie Coleman wasn't. "I can handle that," he said, but he didn't look as if he meant it.

Kiersten started to cry. All of the kids, plus Maurice, sat down on the staircase and stared glumly into the darkness.

They'd tried so hard. They'd accomplished so much. They'd come so far. And now they were trapped in the under-the-bed world forever.

24

Brian hopped to his feet, nearly hitting his head on the tightly shut door under his bed.

"Hey, I've got an idea!" he said. "Follow me."

He darted down the stairs and took off as fast as his legs would carry him to the main directional signpost. Then, with four other children and a monster following him, he ran past city signs. First, there was Philadelphia. No good.

Then, they passed Pittsburgh, Indianapolis, and St. Louis. Kiersten figured it out.

"We've got to make it to California!" she said. "That's Pacific time."

"Yeah, sun's up in St. Louis," Maurice confirmed, glancing above him.

They passed Wichita, Santa Fe, and Phoenix, and finally arrived, breathlessly, on the West Coast.

"Here," Maurice announced. "This'll do. It may be hard to explain, but it'll do!"

Kiersten, Todd, Eric, and Ronnie scrambled up

the stairway to safety. Brian was about to climb up, too, when he turned to say good-bye to Maurice.

"I almost wish I could stay," he said.

"You'd be a hero down here," Maurice told him. "We've hated Snik and Boy for a long time. You made the house land on the wicked witches, you know?"

"You did your part, pal," Brian told Maurice.

"I guess being a pal is what it's all about," Maurice said.

"Yeah, and you know what?' Brian said. "I think you're the best friend I ever had."

"Don't go sentimental on me, kid," Maurice said. "Because you're the ugliest friend I ever had!"

Brian was used to Maurice's teasing now. It didn't bother him. "I'm going to miss you. I really am."

"Why? You going to give up sleeping in a bed?" Maurice asked.

"Nooooo," Brian said thoughtfully.

"So, then I'll be seeing you. Bri, baby, just because you tiptoed down here and threw the wildest bash this town has ever seen doesn't in any way exclude you from catching your share of *trouble*. I kind of liked that trick you pulled with the tomato in the microwave. Does your mom have a microwave?"

"I've already got all the trouble I need," Brian said. "What about my arm? It turned to clothes last night."

"Don't worry. You'll sleep it off. Nothing's permanent unless you're trapped down here. Okay, now, get out of here."

Brian turned to leave, but Maurice called him back one more time.

"Hang on. . . ."

Maurice yanked off his vest and tossed it to Brian. Brian caught it.

"You don't have to — " said Brian, but Maurice cut him off.

"Relax, I'll find another," said Maurice. "Maybe I'll even steal it back from you."

Brian stared at his friend for a moment. Then it was time to go.

Brian climbed the final few steps of the ladder out of the darkness and into the night.

25

Brian caught up with his friends. They had come up under a lounge chair in Malibu, California, and now they were sitting on a deserted beach, watching the morning sky lighten. Everybody was thinking. Nobody was talking.

Brian sank down into the sand and stretched his legs out in front of him. He propped himself up with his elbows. He breathed the fresh air of freedom. He was satisfied with his night's work. He'd saved his little brother. He'd saved all the little monsters from the tyranny of Boy and Snik and the monster guards. Most important, though, he'd made a friend. Maurice had come through for him when the chips were down. Way down.

When the sun was completely up, Brian stood and dusted the sand off his clothes. "I think we'd better find a phone," he told his friends.

There was a road running along the beach. If they followed it, Brian was sure they'd come to a gas station or something with a phone. They'd have a lot of explaining to do to their parents, but they were safe, and that was the most important thing.

Once Brian started thinking about explaining, he realized he had some other explaining to do, too.

"Uh, Kiersten," he said as they walked along. "Your science project . . . and Ronnie, about that tuna fish sandwich?"

Kiersten and Ronnie looked at him and prepared themselves for some interesting news.

"Maurice did it," Brian said. After all, friends were supposed to help one another, weren't they? And Maurice would have done the same for him.